Flash's Cozy Cabin

Charlie Alexander

Flash's Cozy Cabin

Written by Charlie Alexander

Art work by Charlie Alexander

Flash was cutting down the first tree.

He was going to use his new axe!

Stacking the logs was heavy.

But Flash was so excited to clear his land.

Flash needed his ladder.

He was stacking the logs very high.

Be careful up there Flash!

Don't lose your balance!

Flash liked his safety glasses.

He was protecting his eyes.

Flash spent his first day cutting down trees.

Timber!!

It was great to have the land cleared.

What a super job finished!

Flash was lucky to have a little bulldozer.

It made digging a lot easier!

Of course, some digging had to be done by hand.

Flash needed a good shovel.

Landscaping was going well.

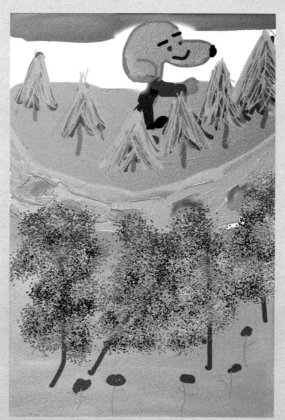

Flash planted some pine trees and some grass.

The new lawn needed to be mowed.

Flash had to work all day to finish!

The cement truck was early.

Flash woke up and was ready to go!

Flash carried the logs to build his cabin.

He was ready to put up the first wall.

The wall was halfway finished.

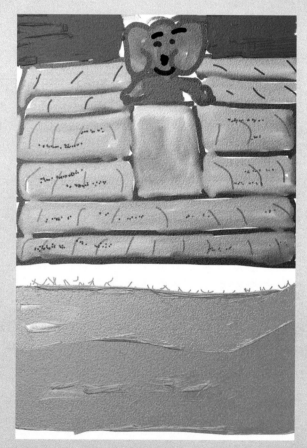

It was time to install the window.

Flash needed lots of nails.

He carried them in a big silver bucket.

Nailing the floor down was rewarding.

Things were coming together.

The roof seemed very high.

Hold on tight Flash!

It was time to finish all the rooms in the cabin.

It was nice to have a good sawhorse.

Lunch was right around the corner.

This made Flash very happy!

Flash planted some beautiful flowers after lunch.

He loves the smell of fresh flowers!

Flash worked on the kitchen next.

The refrigerator fit in perfectly.

The dining room looked awesome.

There were enough chairs for everyone.

The bedroom was inviting.

But it wasn't time to rest yet.

Flash finished the bathroom.

He adjusted the new shower.

A cozy cabin on the lake.

Flash and the duck were home!

Charlie knew where Flash would be.

He knew how dedicated Flash was!

Charlie and Becky came for a visit.

Flash couldn't wait to show off his cozy cabin!

Flash went into the cabin.

He wanted to be sure it was clean so his company
would enjoy themselves.

Ice cream break.

Flash can't resist ice cream!

We all like ice cream!

It was nice of Flash to share.

A boat ride on the lake was so nice!

Too bad it could only be a short ride this time.

Flash had moved all of the furniture for the living room.

He loved the couch.

Flash made sure his car was clean.

His guests might need a ride!

Just a short ride on his bicycle.

Flash had put two new tires on it and he wanted to be
sure it was safe.

Flash was ready to celebrate!

He had built his cozy cabin!!
The End

To order additional copies of this book, contact:
Xlibris
844-714-8691
www.Xlibris.com
Orders@Xlibris.com

ISBN: Softcover   978-1-6698-7566-6
          Hardcover   978-1-6698-7573-4
          EBook   978-1-6698-7565-9

Library of Congress Control Number: 2023908033

Print information available on the last page

Rev. date: 04/26/2023

Printed in the United States
by Baker & Taylor Publisher Services